D1074254

Principal for a Day

by Marisa N. Kossoy

illustrated by Shiela Alejandro

PRINCIPAL

Jackson

© 2020 Marisa N. Kossoy

ISBN 978-1-09834-712-3

All rights reserved.

This book is dedicated to my nephew, Jackson.

May you always remember to be kind, try your best,
work hard, attempt new things, and HAVE FUN!

Jackson snuck a ticket off Mrs. Crowley's desk and wrote his name on it. "Check this out, Giovanni. I'm going to put this in the Principal for a Day box."

"That's a good one," said Giovanni. "Wait till the principal sees it."

By the end of the week, Jackson forgot all about the ticket.
That is until his name was called over the loudspeaker.

"Jackson Stiller, you're this month's Principal for a Day.
Please come to the main office."

Since Jackson never paid attention to announcements, Giovanni nudged him. "That's you! You're Principal for the Day!"

"Huh?" said Jackson.

Jackson dropped the glue he was using to stick Mia's pencil to her desk.

I don't want to be the principal for the day, he thought, walking to the principal's office. That ticket was a stupid idea.

"Good morning," said Principal Pennysworth. "I was pleasantly surprised when I picked this ticket. One of our teachers had to see you being a good school citizen to put your name on it."

"Uh," is all Jackson could say. He thought of all the things he did wrong that month.

"Please come to my office tomorrow at 8 am. We'll help the children to their classroom lines for school arrival."

"Sure," mumbled Jackson.

Kids whizzed past Jackson. "Hey, stop running and get in line."

Principal Pennysworth put her hand on Jackson's shoulder. "That's not how we do it." She talked to the students and they went right to their places.

"How'd you do that?" asked Jackson.

"I told them I needed help and asked if they'd be a role model for the younger students."

Jackson nodded. "Interesting."

After Jackson said the morning announcements, he and the principal made her morning hallway rounds. About to turn a corner, a fifth grader meandered toward them.

"Hey, do you have a pass?" asked Jackson.

Richie eyed Jackson. "How many times do you wander the halls without one?"

Gee whiz, thought Jackson. "Okay, wise guy. Maybe you can get back to your class now."

"Whatever," said Richie, walking away.

"I don't trust him," said Jackson.

"It's okay," said Principal Pennysworth.
"This is typical behavior for Richard."

Wow, thought Jackson, she knows his moves.

"Off to the Kindergarteners," said Principal Pennysworth.
"I scheduled you to read a book to them."

"Good morning, Jackson," said Mrs. Stevens.

Jackson looked around the room. Eager little faces stared at him.
Okay, he thought, I can do this.

KINDER "GARDEN"
WHERE
YOUNG
MINDS
BLO
AN   W!

Halfway through the book, a little girl screamed. "He blew their house down!"

"It's okay," said Jackson, flustered. "Uh, let's just read to the end."

The little girl sniffled.

NUMBERS
2 3 4 5 6 7 8 9 10
11 12 13 14 15 16
17 18 19 20
ART BOARD
My Cat
Karen
Pat
Ron
Rose
Denise
Sadie
Daniel
Stella
Leslie
Frankie
Tom
Austin
Alec
Abigail
Scot
Addison
Laura

Jackson finished the story, emphasizing that the pigs were happy and safe.
He was relieved when the little girl smiled.

Jackson was just as relieved when Principal Pennysworth arrived.
"How'd it go?" she asked.

"Those little kids are sure scary," said Jackson.

Principal Pennysworth laughed. "Off to the auditorium to get everyone involved in our Read-a-thon Fundraiser."

"Huh? I don't participate in those things."

"The fundraisers help pay for new computers and afterschool programs, like last year's soccer training with Coach Fletcher."

"Whoa," said Jackson. "I loved that coach. How can I help?"
"You can talk about the Read-a-thon."

After the principal spoke, she asked Jackson to say a few words.

Jackson gulped. "Hey, guys, you should all participate in the fundraiser."

One of the boys yelled, "You don't participate!"

Gee whiz, busted again, thought Jackson.
"Well, now I know we get stuff with the money
we raise, like books and sports equipment."

Principal Pennysworth patted Jackson
on his back. "You're a natural at this."

"I guess I'm not an example of good behavior,"
said Jackson.

"Every day is a new day, Jackson."

It somehow made Jackson feel better.

"It's on to the cafeteria," said Principal Pennysworth.

As they entered the cafeteria, Liam ran past Landon, knocking the tray out of Landon's hands.

Jackson raced over to help and slipped on the food. "AAHHHHH," he yelled as he went down, butt first.

Everyone laughed until Principal Pennysworth glared around the room.

Jackson headed for Liam. "You almost knocked Landon down."

Liam gave Jackson a side glance.
"You did the same thing to Valentina on Monday."

Busted again, thought Jackson. "Yeah, well I shouldn't have been running either."

Jackson shoved his hands in his pockets and went back to Principal Pennysworth. "Shouldn't Liam sit in your office during recess?"

"It's not necessary. You handled it. Let's go have lunch."

As they ate, the principal handed Jackson a certificate. "You did an amazing job. I'm proud of you."

"Uh, I–I didn't do anything special for that ticket. I–I took it from Mrs. Crowley's desk."

"I know, Jackson," said Principal Pennysworth with a smile.

She really does know everything, he thought.

"You know, Jackson. I think you'd make a fine principal one day."

"Huh? Me? No way. Not me."

The next day, Giovanni whispered, "Hey, let's put one of the frogs in Kimberly's bookbag?"

Jackson thought about it. "It'd sure be funny.
But I'd better not. I may be a principal one day."

THE END